W9-AHT-536

THE
ALIEN
ADVENTURES OF
FINN CASPIAN
THE UNCOMMON COLD

Read more of Finn Caspian's alien adventures!

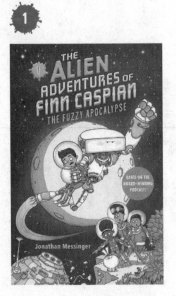

THE ALIEN ADVENTURES OF FINN CASPIAN

THE UNCOMMON COLD

Jonathan Messinger

Illustrated by Aleksei Bitskoff

HARPER

Library of Congress Control Number: 2020944609
ISBN 978-0-06-293221-1 — ISBN 978-0-06-293220-4 (pbk.)

Typography by Jessie Gang
21 22 23 24 25   PC/LSCH   10 9 8 7 6 5 4 3 2 1
❖
First Edition

For Griff, Emers,

and the stomp rockets they rode in on

CONTENTS

One: Breaking News 1

Two: Isolation Vacation 7

Three: Mission Pretty Possible.............19

Four: Robot Reception 28

Five: Metal Paradise 38

Six: Movable Feast 45

Seven: Call a Waambulance 54

Eight: Nowhere to Run to, Baby.............61

Nine: The Plot Sickens..........................68

Ten: Fireworks 74

Eleven: Swarm and Cozy 85

Twelve: Trash Day 94

Thirteen: Long Live the Queen? 101

Fourteen: Friends Don't Let Friends Blow Up 108

Fifteen: Aftershocks 116

A Note About This Story

The tale you are about to read takes place approximately **36.54372 million miles away** from Earth, as the crow flies. It has been collected and woven together via various interview transcripts, recordings, and interstellar **laser screams** sent to Earth from the *Famous Marlowe 280 Interplanetary Exploratory Space Station* over the past decade.

"Laser scream" may be a new term for you, as it is still not well understood on Earth, but we don't have time to get into it here.

The astronauts who boarded the *Marlowe* were charged with **one mission: to discover a planet where humans could one day live**. Captain Isabel Caspian sends out teams of explorers. Finn and his friends are all remarkable, but Finn will always have a special place in the history books.

Because Finn was the first kid born in space.

So in many ways, Finn was born for exactly the type of situation in which we find him here in this book. But it will be up to you to decide if that makes him lucky or not.

HALL OF
EXPLORERS

Abigail Obaro

Troop 301 Captain

Finn Caspian

Chief Detective

Chief Technologist

Sergeant-at-Arms

Robot

Interloper

Chapter One
Breaking News

Finn was just walking out of the library when he saw his three friends heading toward him. Abigail Obaro, his best friend, was in front. Behind her strode Elias Carreras and Vale Gil. Together the four of them made up Explorers Troop 301, and they had explored some crazy planets together. They were an amazing team.

But right now, something was different. As

his friends approached, Finn could tell they weren't on his team. It was the three of them, and the one of him.

"Uh, hey," said Finn, as the other three got closer. "What's up, guys?"

Abigail nodded and turned back to Elias and Vale.

No one said anything. No one did anything. It was silent in the hallway of the *Famous Marlowe 280 Interplanetary Exploratory Space Station.*

"So I got some new books out of the li—" said Finn.

"Cool," said Elias. He didn't seem to even notice he'd cut Finn off. "We, uh, we should get going."

"Yeah, cool," said Vale. "Super cool. See you later."

His three friends spread out to go around him. Finn held out his arms to stop them, and they all jumped back.

"Back, foul demon!" shouted Vale.

"Foul demon?" said Finn. "Vale, did you eat too much astronaut ice cream again? Actually, all three of you guys are being really weird. What's up?"

The three of them looked at each other.

"Nothing," said Abigail.

"That was the least convincing 'nothing' I've ever heard," said Finn. "You might as well have just said, 'I'm lying.' Obviously, something is going on."

Elias shrugged.

"It's not really a big deal," he said.

"I'm sure she's going to be fine," said Abigail.

Vale put his hand over his face.

"There it is," he said. "Cat's out of the bag."

"What is it?" asked Finn. "You're sure who's going to be fine? Is someone not fine right now? Is it Paige?"

Paige was Finn's little sister. And she was super talented at getting into trouble.

"No!" Abigail exclaimed, seeming relieved. "No, of course not. Paige is totally fine."

"Oh, good," said Finn.

"Well, I guess that's it then," said Elias. "See you, Finn!"

"No!" said Finn. "Who are you guys talking about if it's not Paige?"

"Eh, forget it," said Abigail.

"I can't forget it!" Finn shouted. "Like you

guys said, the cat's out of the bag!"

"Just put the cat back in the bag," said Vale.

"I can't!" said Finn. "The cat's out and is now scurrying down the hallway."

"I don't know," said Elias. "The cat seems kind of sleepy to me. She might want to go back in the bag and rest."

"The cat ate like fifteen candy bars and is bouncing off the walls," said Finn.

"I think the cat loves bags," said Abigail. "And just needs to find the right bag to settle down in—"

"Cats hate bags!" shouted Finn. "This cat thinks bags are bad. Bad bags!"

"Your mom is a snot monster!" yelled Vale.

And with that, Finn slumped against the wall, hand over his heart.

"She is?" he said.

Abigail nodded, but didn't come near him.

"So that means," said Finn, "I'm going to be a snot monster, too."

All three of Finn's friends nodded and took a step away from him.

"Sorry about that whole cat thing," said Abigail. "But, you know, not sorry enough to give you a hug over it or anything."

Chapter Two
Isolation Vacation

No one likes getting a cold. No matter where someone is in the universe, the symptoms are the same: runny nose, watery eyes, cough, sore throat, the redness on that little part of the face where the nostrils meet the upper lip (that's the worst).

But on a space station, a common cold can

be a disaster. Every breath you take on a space station, someone else has already taken it. You're just borrowing that bit of air until you puff it out of your lungs for someone else to inhale and use for a second. And with all that air swapping comes germ swapping.

Of course, the *Marlowe* has excellent air filtration systems, but a cold virus is the trickiest life-form in the known universe. The cold is basically a biological ninja, sneaking in and side-kicking your sinuses no matter what defenses you've put up.

So it's a policy on the *Marlowe* that if any astronaut gets sick, their whole family must be quarantined immediately. Quarantine is like being grounded. You have to stay in your room, no one can come visit you, and the only people you can talk to are the ones in your family.

It's punishment by boredom, even though

you didn't do anything wrong.

If you're a little sick, you may only have to be quarantined for a couple days. If your cough never stops, you'll be quarantined for a week or two. If you are, as Vale said, a "snot monster," you could be in your tiny compartment with just your family for as long as a month, until everyone is cleared.

"Thith will be fun," said Finn's mom, Isabel Caspian, the *Marlowe* captain. Her cold had so filled her sinuses with snot that she sounded like her head was inside a pumpkin. "Don't be tho thad, Finn. It will path by before you know it. Who wanth to play Monopoly?"

And so the Caspian family—mother Isabel, father Leon, son Finn, and daughter Paige— began playing their first of many games of Monopoly.

"It's not fair that I have to be here even though I'm not sick," said Finn.

"Yeah," said Paige. "You guys are all gross and sick and I'm fine. Also, it's not fair that you make me be the thimble in Monopoly. Who wants to be a thimble? What even is a thimble?"

But of course, by the next day, both Finn and Paige were full-fledged snot monsters.

A few times a day, every day, Captain Caspian would sit at a computer in their family's living room, going over reports on the *Marlowe*'s travels and sending advice and commands to the rest of the ship. The space station outside the Caspian compartment continued to make its way across galaxies, even though the four snot monsters couldn't see it.

Foggy, Finn's robot, got to come and go as he pleased. The entire family would have to huddle in Finn's parents' bedroom, door closed, so Foggy could open and shut the front door without letting out contaminants. Sometime in the third week, it got a little old.

"Hello, Caspian family!" Foggy yelled from the hallway. "Please exit the living room so I may come in."

"Ugh," said Paige, putting down a crayon. "Let's drop everything. Finn's sidekick wants to come in . . . *again*."

The family got up, retreated to the parents' bedroom, and shut the door—as they did every time Foggy came to visit.

"Tell Foggy he can come in, Finn," said Captain Caspian.

"All clear," mumbled Finn.

"You have to yell it, Finn," said Captain Caspian. "He's not going to hear you."

Truthfully, Finn didn't want to yell it. Foggy was always so upbeat. Sometimes when he was sick, Finn just wanted to feel miserable.

"All clear!" Finn shouted. They heard the front door open and close, and they all filed out into the living room.

"Hello, Caspian family!" said Foggy.

"You already said that," said Finn.

"I am so pleased to see you!" shouted Foggy. "Even though I am not pleased to see you looking so terrible. I wish I could help you all. I'm sad you're all feeling so bad. If there's anything I can do, please tell me."

"I still can't believe you choose to come in here with us," said Paige. "There's no way I'd volunteer to hang out with Finn every day."

Finn considered which Monopoly piece to throw at his sister.

"But he is my boon companion!" Foggy exclaimed. "My true pal. My friend-to-the-end! There is no way I would ever abandon him here to his snot monstrosity!"

"Foggy, please," said Finn. "A little less loud."

"I am sorry," said Foggy. "Robots, as you know, cannot get sick."

"Yes, you've said that," said Finn.

"So, I do not know what it feels like to be sick," said Foggy.

"I know," said Finn.

"So while you are wretched, I will just observe you, so I may learn about what being sick means," said Foggy.

He sat down on the coffee table across from Finn and stared at him as Finn pushed a tissue up his nose.

"You have a little flag dangling from your nostril, Finn," said Foggy.

"It's not a flag, Foggy, it's a—"

"I have an idea!" shouted Foggy. He sprang to his feet. "Dance party!"

Foggy pushed a button on his left arm and

music began playing out of his torso. He started twirling his hips and pointing his finger in the air. He looked like he would tip over at any second.

"Foggy, please!" shouted Finn. "I don't feel well. I don't want to talk. I don't want to move. And I definitely don't want to dance."

"Yeah, none of us want to see that, either," said Paige.

Finn coughed and spittle flew out of his mouth all over Foggy's chest.

"Ew," said Finn. "Sorry, Foggy."

"It's okay," said Foggy. "I'm sure it's harmless."

"Do you want a tissue?" asked Finn.

Foggy looked at the one dangling from Finn's nose and shook his head.

"Definitely not," he said. "Let me just run a cleaning program. One moment."

Foggy beeped and whirred. A small squeegee

emerged from his side. It wiped up Finn's spit and returned to his body.

"There," said Foggy. "Now I won't spread those germs throughout the *Marlowe*."

"Are you leaving?" asked Finn. He was in a bad mood and wanted a little space.

"No way," said Foggy. "I have lots more observations to make!"

He sat down and stared hard at Finn. For a long time.

"Um, you know what, Foggy?" said Finn. "You can go. Please. Feel free."

"Okay," said Foggy. "If that would make you feel better."

"It would," said Finn.

Foggy stood up, knocking over the

Monopoly board as he made his way toward the door.

"Oh, so sorry," he said.

The family all looked at him.

"I. . . I had all the railroads," said Finn.

"I'm sorry for the trouble," said Foggy. "But could you please?"

He pointed to the bedroom door. Every Caspian in the room sighed. They slowly walked toward the bedroom.

"It's not fair," Paige whined.

"It's definitely not fun," said her dad.

"Finn, you really shouldn't talk to Foggy that way," said Captain Caspian.

"But he was staring at me," said Finn.

"You know you're very lucky to have him," she said. "He's a good friend to you, and there are millions of kids on Earth who would die to have their own ro—"

"Um, excuse me, Caspian family," said

Foggy. "Could you please close the door? So I can leave? It's awkward to stand here and listen to you."

Captain Caspian closed the door and Finn flopped on his parents' bed. No one heard Foggy stifle a small, robotic cough as he left.

Chapter Three
Mission Pretty Possible

"Finn! You're alive!" shouted Vale as he ran down the hall. Finn had just taken his first step out of his compartment.

"Yep!" said Finn. "Four weeks, three days, seven hours, thirty-five minutes, and let's call it an even thirty seconds since I was quarantined."

"Sorry I called your mom a snot monster!" said Vale.

"What was that, Vale?" said Captain Caspian, following Finn out into the hall.

"Um," said Vale. "I said, I'm sorry I called your mom *not*-a-monster. Finn was calling you a snot monster. Right, Finn? And then I was saying, 'no, she's *not* a monster.' That may have sounded like 'snot monster,' but it was 'snot a monster.'"

"So if you were defending me, why were you apologizing?" said Captain Caspian. She smiled at Finn. She knew that she made Vale nervous, and she was enjoying this.

"I wasn't!" said Vale. Sweat rained off his forehead. "I wasn't saying, 'I'm sorry,' like, 'my mistake.' I was saying, 'I'm sorry,' like, 'No way. Nuh-uh, Finn Caspian. Excuse me? I'm sorry, you are NOT going to call your mother a snot monster in front of me! I'm sorry, but that is *not* okay.'"

Captain Caspian was laughing hard enough now that Vale realized she was just joking with him.

"Oh, I see," said Vale. "You guys get locked up together for a month and all you do is plan a joke on me?"

"Vale!!" Foggy came bounding out of the compartment. "Ah, my dear old friend, Vale! Oh, how I've missed you!"

He picked up Vale in a bear hug.

"Thanks?" said Vale. "Finally someone misses me. And it's the weird robot who saw me yesterday."

"We all missed you, Vale," said Captain Caspian. "And I'll miss you even more when you go out on your new mission!"

"What?" asked Finn. "Really?!"

"Yes," she said. "While we've all been cooped up for the last few weeks, I've been planning the next Explorers Troop 301 mission. Vale, why don't you go get Elias and Abigail and tell them to meet us in the map room. Finn, you and Foggy come with me."

Vale ran off to get them.

"Finn, I want to talk to you before the others arrive," said Captain Caspian. "I hope you'll take this mission seriously."

"I take every mission seriously, Mom," said Finn.

"I know, but this one is especially for you," she said.

Finn tilted his head. "What do you—"

"Here are the sickos!" Vale yelled as he ran in with Abigail and Elias.

"I missed you guys!" Finn hugged them both. "No germs, I promise."

"Just your usual germs, you mean," said Abigail.

Everyone got quiet. That's what it was like in the map room. Something about the place made the explorers feel like they should be subdued.

The room was round, dark, and had a domed ceiling. On the walls were maps of planets *Marlowe* explorers had ventured to in the past. In the center of the room a projector rose out of the floor. It shone a giant map of Galaxy Fishbone on the ceiling. (The *Marlowe* had long since run out of names for all the galaxies they visited, so Paige got to name this one.) At the center of the map was a bright red star. About fifteen planets surrounded it. They were all different colors.

"It's incredible," said Abigail.

"It is," said Captain Caspian.

Captain Caspian pressed a button on the console in front of the projector, and fourteen planets shrunk away. The image of a blue world, seven planets from the star, grew on the ceiling.

"That's it," said Captain Caspian. "That's where you'll be going."

"What is it?" asked Elias.

"We don't know the name, but we do know that it seems peaceful," she said. "There's no reason to think anything down there would want to hurt us." She had said this to them

before. And every time she said it, she'd been wrong.

"Any*thing*?" said Elias. "I thought we tried not to call aliens 'things' because it made them seem like objects."

"You're right," said Captain Caspian. "But those aren't aliens living down there. They're robots."

"Robots?" said Foggy.

"Yes," said Captain Caspian.

"Only robots?" asked Foggy.

"Yes," said Captain Caspian. "It's really unusual. As far as we can tell, it's all robots. It's time to visit a planet of some metal beings just like you, Foggy. You've been cooped up with us sick humans long enough."

"Amazing!" yelled Foggy. "I'm positively delighted! Cough, cough!"

"Did you just cough?" said Finn.

"No," said Foggy. "Don't be silly! Off to the robot planet!"

"Hold on," said Abigail. "Normally we look for planets where humans could live. Why are we going to this one if it's all robots?"

"You're right," said Captain Caspian. "We don't think this planet is for humans, since there are no life-forms other than the robots and it's very cold out there. But we would really like to understand how such a planet came to be."

"Oh, this is gonna be awesome!" shouted Elias. "I wonder if they'll let me take any robots apart to see how they work."

"I don't think so," laughed Captain Caspian. "But I'm glad to see you're excited. We should all appreciate how wonderful robots are."

Captain Caspian looked at Finn. Finn knew she meant him.

"Perfect," said Foggy. "Tallyho, let's go, pip pip, cough cough."

"Did you just cough again?" said Finn.

But Foggy didn't answer. He was already gone. He'd flown down to the explorer pod bay and was already sitting in the tiny ship that would take the explorers down to the planet. Seat belt fastened.

Chapter Four
Robot Reception

"Huh," said Abigail. She peered out the explorer pod window. They were just entering the atmosphere of the planet below.

"What is it?" said Elias. "Please tell me nothing bad."

"Nothing bad," said Abigail. "Definitely weird. But I'm still going with nothing bad."

Finn strained to see out the window, as well.

In the distance, he could see what looked like a small village. But right below them, outside a big stone building, a group of robots stood looking up at the ship.

"What's so weird about that?" said Finn. "They're just there to welcome us. My mom sent a signal down. They know we're coming."

"Sure," said Abigail. "But . . . wait a second."

"Oh, I can't wait!" said Foggy. He'd already unbuckled and was pressed against the window.

Finn watched as the robots moved, all at once. There were maybe twenty metal creatures on the surface of the planet, all of them human-oid. They shuffled around until they formed a circle. Then, at the same time, they all raised their right arms, one finger pointing to the sky.

"Are they pointing at us?" asked Finn.

"Wait for it," said Abigail.

Then the robots danced. There was no other way to describe it. They shook it to the left.

They shook it to the right. They all moved in unison, arms waving, legs kicking, robot hips swinging like no one was watching.

Finn and Abigail laughed.

"What is it?" asked Elias, who was seated in the back of the pod. "I can't see."

"They're dancing," said Finn.

"Specifically, I think they're doing some kind of Hokey Pokey," said Abigail.

"Ah yes, the universal dance," said Foggy. He could barely contain his excitement to meet his fellow robots.

Abigail tried to land the pod a safe distance from the robots, but as their ship got closer to the ground, the robots fanned out. They seemed to want the ship to land in the middle of their circle.

"Um, generally it's not a good idea to run toward a landing spacecraft," said Abigail. "I don't want to squash any bots."

"Oh, you won't," said Foggy. "We are far too intelligent for that."

"We?" said Finn. "Aren't you one of us?"

The pod jerked as Abigail touched down. When Finn looked up, Explorers Troop 301 was surrounded.

Foggy was the first off the ship.

"Hallo, new friends!" he shouted as he landed on the flat, rocky surface of the planet. The ground was shiny and marbled, like a kitchen counter. "We come in peace!"

"The captain is supposed to make the first greeting," grumbled Abigail. "But I guess you can have this one, Foggy."

The robots didn't respond, but they did start dancing again. The circle drew tighter as the robots closed in on the ship. They snapped their fingers and shimmied toward the explorers as each astronaut disembarked.

"I'm Abigail Obaro, captain of Explorers

Troop 301," shouted Abigail. "We come from the *Famous Marlowe 280 Interplanetary Exploratory Space Station*. We mean you no harm."

The robots' dance became simpler as they got closer. Now they were doing a very basic Running Man, arms and legs pumping up and down.

"Should we be worried?" whispered Elias.

The robots were now just a few yards from the explorers.

"Why aren't they saying anything?" Finn asked.

Now the robots were just a few feet away.

"We come in peace!" Foggy shouted again. He was boogying as best he could in response.

The robots continued to close in on them. Finn could feel sweat bead inside his helmet.

"This is not good," whispered Abigail.

"There's no music," said Elias. "Who dances to no music? This is creepy."

The explorers pressed into each other. The robots came closer.

"I got this," said Vale. "Leave it to me."

Vale Gil, the troop's sergeant-at-arms, had spent the most time in combat training. He stepped in front of his friends.

"Here we go," he said.

"Vale, be careful!" shouted Abigail.

Vale bent his elbows, raised both hands, and faced the closest robots. Confronted with a horde of twenty robots closing in

on him, Vale did the only thing he could think to do.

He danced.

Vale began to perform the worst robot dance you've ever seen. His legs and arms pumped up and down as Vale jerked his body left, right, and forward. He slid, he shimmied.

"Uh," said Vale. "Uh. Yeah. Uh."

The robots stopped advancing. They all stood and watched Vale. Vale barely noticed. He was so impressed with his own moves.

"Come on," said Vale. "Join the party!"

Reluctantly, all the explorers began dancing their own version of the robot dance.

They were on a new planet. They were millions of light-years from Earth. And yet here they were, mechanically raising and lowering their arms, dancing to no music.

"Loosen up, Elias!" shouted Foggy. "It's all in the hips!"

One robot stepped forward.

"You," said the robot. It pointed at Foggy. "You are like us. Yet you are with them."

"Yes," said Foggy. "And we are so happy to be here."

"We are happy to have you here," said the robot. "I am called 2111222111122121222."

"Nice to meet you, 2111222111122121222," said Foggy. "My name is Foggy. These are my friends, Finn, Abigail, Elias, and Vale."

"Why are they still dancing?" asked 2111222111122121222.

The astronauts had been too nervous to stop. But now they all felt silly. They awkwardly stopped dancing, as if someone had suddenly stopped the music.

"Better," said 2111222111122121222. "That was not good dancing."

"Hey!" said Vale.

"Except you," said 2111222111122121222. It pointed at Vale. "You got the moves."

"I *knew* it!" said Vale, pumping a fist.

"Come with us, Foggy and friends. We invite you to our homes."

Chapter Five
Metal Paradise

The robot known as 2111222111122121222 walked beside Foggy, the kids trailing closely. The rest of the robots had dispersed in different directions. Finn figured they must have all gone to their robot homes.

"How many of you are there?" Finn heard Foggy ask 2111222111122121222 as they walked. "I counted twenty-three back there, including yourself."

"Yes, there are twenty-three like me," said the robot. "But there are many more not like me."

"Do you mean there are different types of robots on this planet?" asked Elias. As the chief technologist of the troop, Elias was the biggest robot fan. He'd tried to build his own robots in the past. And while he hadn't pulled it off just yet, he had a notebook full of designs.

"Of course," said 2111222111122121222. "Just like I'm sure there are many different types of whatever you are wherever you come from. Just today, I've spoken with a number of different friends, including 1112212121212, and 22221111221212121222. And do you know what 22212121111111 said to me just this morning?"

"Nope!" said Vale.

"She told me 111222121222221112212 was going to kick 121212122222121222 out of his house if 121212122222121222 didn't just admit that 111222121222221112212 was a better dancer."

2111222111122121222 laughed. Foggy joined in.

"Ha!" he said. "Ho ho ha. That is so 111222121222221112212."

"Isn't it?" said 2111222111122121222.

"You all have names like that?" asked Vale. "Just ones and twos?

"Yes," said their robot host. "It is very efficient."

"How do you remember them all, though?" asked Vale.

"Oh, we have a trick," said 211122211112121222. "For instance, 111222121222221112212 has one dimple on his face, one scratch on his arm, one antenna on his head, two eyes, two feet, two hands, one neck, two lights on his head, one light on his foot,

two buttons on his chest, two buttons on his back, two wheels under his left foot (but you can't really see them, so that's not that helpful), two wheels under his right foot (but you can't really see—"

"Please stop," said Vale. "My human brain hurts."

"You could just call him Lou," said 2111222111122121222. "He prefers that. Most of us have nicknames we've given ourselves."

"Do you have one?" said Vale.

"Yes," said 2111222111122121222. "I call myself SuperAwesome."

"Oh," laughed Vale. "I guess if I could name myself, I'd call myself SuperAwesome, too."

"You would actually be KindofAwesome, since I am SuperAwesome," said Super-Awesome. "Now, let's go inside, shall we?"

"And that guy called himself Lou?" laughed Vale. "Why would—"

"Shhh, Vale," hissed Foggy as SuperAwesome went ahead, entering a large stone building. "Don't embarrass me."

"Vale is just joking around, Foggy," said Finn. "Robots can take a joke, can't they?"

Foggy rolled his eyes.

"Just let me do the talking," he said. "Cough cough, cough cough, spittle."

"What did you just say?" asked Finn.

"I said just let me do the talking," said Foggy.

"No, after that," said Finn. "Did you cough? Foggy, are you sick?"

"Gah," said Foggy. "That's such a human way to think. Of course I'm not sick. Robots can't catch colds, Finn. Wise up!"

Foggy hurried to catch up to Super-Awesome.

"Was that weird to any of you guys?" asked Finn.

"Very," said Elias. "Something isn't right with Foggy."

"Right?" said Finn. "He's never been that rude to me before. He's always been just happy to be my friend."

"No, I meant the coughing," said Elias.

"Oh, yeah," said Finn. "That, too."

Chapter Six
Movable Feast

"And so then 2121212211221212222222111 said, 'Give me a break! At least I'm not a part of the 1111111 generation!'"

SuperAwesome slapped the table, laughing hard at her own joke.

The explorers were sitting around a large, rectangular stone table. SuperAwesome sat at the head of it. Seated beside her was Foggy, laughing just as hard as she was. Around the table were all kinds of robots. Some were as small as ants, some were as round as bowling balls, some looked like walking fish. Others were more like Foggy and SuperAwesome: they had heads, arms, and legs like humans.

All the robots had been called together for this dinner to welcome the explorers. Except there wasn't any food served. The bots were plugged into outlets wired into the table. Apparently, the electricity at this particular table was delicious, because the robots seemed to be having the time of their lives. The explorers sat together, silent, confused, and hungry.

"Do you have any food?" said Vale. "I'm hungry and I was always told not to stick my mouth on electrical outlets."

"Hahaha," laughed SuperAwesome and several of the other robots. "We have heard of this! You require 'food' to keep going. You creatures with bodies are so funny, aren't you? Here, let's see if we have some 'food' for you."

Every time SuperAwesome said the word "food," it sounded like she thought it was the funniest word in the universe. A handful of robots fell out of their chairs at the mention of the word.

"Tell me, Foggy," said SuperAwesome. "How are you able to stand it, being with these funny little fleshy creatures all the time?"

"Oh, it's not so bad," said Foggy. "You get used to their weird habits."

"Not so bad?!" shouted Finn. "Foggy, we're your family."

"Family?" asked SuperAwesome, sounding scandalized. "Do you— Ah, never mind, here is your food."

A tall, round robot with a tray balanced on one hand entered the room. He lowered the tray onto the table in front of the astronauts.

On it was a very neatly arranged pyramid of smooth, rectangular stones.

"There you are," said SuperAwesome. "Food for our flesh friends."

The explorers were aghast. Foggy shifted uncomfortably.

"I don't mean to be rude, SuperAwesome," said Abigail. "But this isn't food for humans. If we try to bite into any of these rocks, we'll break our teeth."

SuperAwesome took in this information as though she were reading the newspaper.

"Foggy, tell me, are they always like this?"

"Not all the time," said Foggy. "But you should try being in the same room with them for a month straight. It's no electricity picnic like we have here I can tell you that cough cough."

"I bet," said SuperAwesome.

"Foggy," said Finn. "Could I speak to you alone for a minute?"

Foggy sighed and made a show of slowly getting up from the table. He walked out the door and Finn joined him outside, on the smooth stone courtyard of SuperAwesome's home. The light from the planet's star glinted pink on the ground.

"What is going on with you?" asked Finn.

"Oh, I'm sorry, Finn," said Foggy. "I know I'm not being a berry good friend. But I want dose robots in dere to like me, and it seemth like they don't like you very much. Tho for jutht thith one planet, can I be a little rude to you?"

"First of all, no, that's not how friendship works," said Finn. "If you're my friend, then you have to be my friend all the time. But that's not what I meant. Why do you keep saying 'cough cough'? And you sound weird. I'm worried about you."

Foggy shuffled his feet and looked down.

"It's nothing cough cough," he said. "It's jutht a little habig I picked up, cough cough cough *CUFFWAWFF*, cough."

"It sounds like you're sick," said Finn.

"Ha, that's ridiculouth," said Foggy. "I'm a robot, I can't get sick."

"I know, but what else could it be?" said Finn. "I think we should pack up here and go back to the *Marlowe* to get you checked out. It's not like humans could ever live here anyway. The only food they have are those rocks that are hard as . . . um . . . rocks."

Foggy let out a loud electronic hiss that sounded like *SKROOOONNNNKK*.

"Did you just clear your throat?" asked Finn.

"No," said Foggy. "I'm perfectly fine. And all our travels are all about humans. Finally we find a planet with some of my fellow robots, and you want to leave right away."

"Foggy, our mission is to find a planet where humans could one day live," said Finn.

"But your mother said the mission on this planet is to better appreciate robots," said Foggy.

"I appreciate *you*, Foggy," said Finn. "But these other robots . . ."

"My mission, right now, is to go back in with my robot friends, plug in for a delicious dinner, and have a few laughs cough cough *CUFFAWFF* puke."

A little spark flew out of Foggy's mouth and died in the air.

"Foggy," said Finn.

"It's nothing!" said Foggy. He marched back into SuperAwesome's building.

"Now, where were we?" said Foggy.

"You were telling us cough cough *CUF-FAWFF*," said SuperAwesome.

"Oh, right," said Foggy. "COUGH COUGH COUGH *BLECH*."

Foggy fell over, clanging on the stone floor.

"Foggy!" shouted Finn.

"Leave him alone," said SuperAwesome. "Let one of us take care of him. COUGH COUGH *CUFFAWFF*."

"No, he's my friend!" shouted Finn.

"2221121222, 121111212121, and 12222122222, please escort these *humans* outside," said SuperAwesome.

Before Finn could say another word, three big, round-shouldered robots had grabbed Abigail, Elias, and Vale and yanked them out of their seats. There was nothing Finn could do as they were all ushered back outside.

"FOGGY!" yelled Finn.

"Goodbye, humans!" called SuperAwesome. "Don't bother coming back!"

Chapter Seven
Call a Waambulance

"Ugh, I don't like that SuperAwesome and her 12121222s or whatever," said Abigail. "You'd think that someone who coordinates a big welcome dance like that would be a much nicer person."

"She's not a person," said Vale. "That's the problem. They're all just a bunch of robots."

"Hey, so is Foggy," said Finn. "It doesn't

matter that they're robots. We need to help Foggy, and I'm guessing we're going to need to help them, too."

"Yeah, I'm with Finn," said Elias. "Just because someone is a robot doesn't mean they don't have a heart."

"I'm going to let that one go," said Abigail. "Okay, so what's up with Foggy, and how do we help him?"

Finn told his friends about his conversation with Foggy, and the spark that had flown out of Foggy's mouth.

"I know this sounds weird," said Finn, "but I think he's sick."

"Robots don't have hearts," said Vale. "And robots don't get sick."

"But robots can get a virus," said Elias. His three friends all looked at him like he'd just declared his name was 1212222122.

Elias explained that computers and robots

can't get sick like humans do. A human usually gets sick from germs or viruses: little microscopic organisms that invade humans. They get into their noses or mouths, and sometimes into their blood.

"Gross!" said Vale. "I'm never breathing again."

"You should also start washing your hands

more," said Elias. "But that's a story for a different time."

He went on to say that germs can't hurt computers. Without a living organism, the germ or virus can't survive. But a "virus" for a computer is a completely different problem. Computers run on their own language: a code. And if there's something wrong in the code—either a bad piece of code was slipped onto the computer, or a piece of code on the computer got broken—then that computer could get a virus.

"So something broke inside of Foggy?" said Finn.

"That's my guess," said Elias.

"It must have happened when he visited you guys in quarantine," said Abigail.

"The cleaning program," said Finn. "He ran a cleaning program when I spit on him!"

"Ew," said Abigail. "You spit on him?!"

"No, I coughed and got spit on him," said Finn.

"Oh, yeah, way better," said Abigail. She took one step away from Finn.

"Dude, you don't cough into your elbow?" said Vale. "It's like I hardly know you."

"But Elias said a sick human couldn't give a virus to a computer," said Finn.

"Right," said Elias. "So who knows how this happened?"

The explorers all stood in silence, thinking about how to solve this problem.

"Well, whatever happened, it seems like Foggy is contagious," said Elias. "SuperAwesome sounded SuperGross when we left."

Finn put his hand on Elias's shoulder.

"So if the problem is with Foggy's code," said Finn, "do you think you could fix it? If we got Foggy alone?"

Elias shrugged.

"Maybe."

"Okay," said Finn. "Great. All we have to do is go in there and convince SuperAwesome to give us back Foggy, and then we can see what's wrong with him."

"Why don't you just ask SuperAwesome right now?" said Vale. He pointed at the robot stumbling out of the building.

"What have you done?" asked Super-Awesome. The robot lurched toward Finn. Finn jumped back just in time. SuperAwesome fell to the ground.

"You," said the robot. "You did this COUGH *CRAFFLOFF* puke puke *blech*."

Two sparks and a little bit of sizzled wire flew out of SuperAwesome's mouth as the robot's eyes closed. She lay still.

"Oh boy," said Abigail.

"They've done this to her!" shouted a robotic voice inside the building. "Get them!"

The three tall, round-shouldered robots came bounding out of the building.

"Fun times," said Vale.

"Hope you're feeling one hundred percent, Finn," said Abigail. "Because I think we need to run at about one hundred miles per hour."

Chapter Eight
Nowhere to Run to, Baby

The four explorers ran as fast as they could toward their explorer pod. They were lucky that the robots chasing them weren't particularly speedy.

"If we climb in there," shouted Abigail, pointing at the pod, "those robots will just pry the ship open. They could really damage it."

"Okay," said Finn. "Then let's run past it and make our way to the next building. We can try to lose them over there."

The explorers all ran straight past their ship to the village of small buildings just beyond it. Finn had spied it from the explorer pod but hadn't thought of it again until now. They ran through the narrow alleys of the town—robots apparently didn't need cars, so there were no streets—and tried their best to go unnoticed.

The alleys were teeming with robots of every different shape and size. Finn accidentally stepped on a few tiny ones, but they seemed designed to recover quickly.

"Sorry!" Finn would shout, but the tiny robots would just pop back up into their proper form and wave their hands. It was like Finn stomping on them was nothing more than a bit of rain.

The guards spotted them, and the explorers dove deeper into the maze of alleys in this village. Vale noticed a bucket full of black goop and knocked it over as they ran past.

The guards slowed down and walked carefully through the goop, like it was glue that was going to dry and trap them in place.

"Okay," said Finn as they dodged around another corner. "I think we've lost them."

"What are you?" asked a round robot flying just over the explorers' heads.

"We're robots!" shouted Elias, stepping forward. "Newest models. Never seen anything like it. Can't keep us on the shelves!"

"Robots?" said the flying bot. It stuck out a small stone wand and poked Vale in the shoulder. "You're awfully squishy."

Vale grabbed the wand out of the robot's hand and poked it back.

"And you're a little too pokey!" shouted Vale.

The bot spun away from the explorers and caught sight of the three tall robots making their way through the crowded alleys.

"Over here!" shouted the
flying bot. "Guards, guards!
They're over here!"

"Snitch," said Vale.

"Squishy," said the flying bot.

The explorers turned down an alley. It was a dead end. Nothing but smooth, shiny stone walls. Behind them, the guards blocked the only way out.

"What have you done to Queen 2111222111122121222?" asked the first guard to step into the alley.

"She's your queen?" asked Abigail. "So the robot who was frazzing out back there was . . . your . . . queen?"

"Answer us!" shouted the second guard bot as they stalked closer to the kids. Finn, Elias, Abigail, and Vale pressed their backs against the wall.

"Yeah!" said the third guard. "Cough cough puke *blech blurp*."

The guard fell over, a drip of oil spilling from his mouth. The other two guards made equally gross sounds and keeled over, forming a guard pile in the middle of the alleyway.

"Um, what do we do now?" asked Vale.

A door opened beside the explorers.

"Come on, in here." It was the flying bot. "This is my house. Bring them inside."

"Why should we trust you?" asked Vale.

"Because those are three of the queen's guards," said the robot. "And the second anyone sees them lying on the ground, you can bet another hundred will be on their way."

"Yeah, but you could be a spy for the queen," said Vale.

"*You* could be a spy for the queen!" shouted the robot.

"Oh wow," said Vale. "I never thought of that. You're kind of blowing my mind."

"We are not spies!" shouted Elias. "And here's hoping you aren't, either. Thank you for your help. I accept on behalf of my friends."

"Don't thank me yet," said the robot. "You guys have to carry those suckers in here."

Finn watched as Abigail, Elias, and Vale each grabbed a guard by the feet.

"Oh, come on," said Abigail. "You're not sick anymore. Grab a robot head and help."

Chapter Nine
The Plot Sickens

"My name is Luxor," said the robot, after the explorers had dragged the three guards inside. "I'm not going to bother to tell you my number name because I was stripped of it long ago."

Luxor told the explorers he had once worked for the queen, but after a disagreement with her over the proper way to dance the cha-cha, Luxor was thrown out of the imperial court.

"That's why you snitched on us," said Vale. "So you could get back in SuperAwesome's good graces."

"Yes, that's true," said Luxor. "But please. That's Queen SuperAwesome to you."

"*Queen* SuperAwesome!" exclaimed Vale. "That has to be the best name ever. I still can't believe that guy called himself Lou."

"You guys met Lou?" asked Luxor. "How is that old bag of bolts, anyway?"

The explorers shrugged. They didn't know if Lou had caught the virus or not.

"Never mind," said Luxor. "The point is that when Queen SuperAwesome threw me out, I lost touch with all my friends. They turned their backs on me. I never thought that would happen. And the last thing I need is word getting around that I had a pile of the queen's guards outside my door."

"Thank you for your help," said Abigail. "I

am Abigail Obaro. I'm the captain of Explorers Troop 301. We're visiting from the *Marlowe 280 Interplanetary Exploratory Space Station*."

"Fancy," said Luxor.

"Thanks?" said Abigail. "We had a robot friend with us. He became fast friends with Super—the queen. But he got sick."

"Ha!" said Luxor. "Robots can't get sick."

"Sure can," said Vale. "Elias, tell him everything."

"They can get viruses or glitches in their software," Elias explained. He told Luxor what they had seen happen to Foggy and then to the queen, too.

"And now, apparently, these guards," said Finn. "Elias, do you think you can see what's wrong with them? Maybe if we can figure out what's happening, we can fix Foggy and the queen."

"Wait, you brought a bunch of virus-infected

guards into my home?" said Luxor.

"You told us to!" said Vale.

"Don't worry," said Elias. "My theory is that the virus spread when all those robots plugged in at dinner. Luxor, so long as you don't connect to the guards, you should be fine."

"Okay," said Luxor. "But just in case . . ."

Luxor placed blankets over the guards.

"That's . . . not . . . ," said Elias. "Why do you even have blankets? You know what, never mind. I need to take one blanket off so I can check out this guard."

Elias knelt down and found a panel on the back of the robot. He pried it open, exposing the robot's circuitry.

Elias tapped some numbers on a keypad in the robot's back. A long string of numbers raced past on a small screen.

"I can't look," said Luxor. "I think I'm going to be sick!"

"Is it that bad?" said Finn.

"Well, it's not going to be easy," said Elias.

"Okay," said Finn. "Elias, you work on that. I'm going back to the queen's house."

"Are you crazy?" said Vale. "Don't you remember that we were chased out of there and basically blamed for taking down the queen of the entire planet?"

"Yep," said Finn. "But that's where Foggy is."

"So that's where we'll go," said Abigail.

Finn shook his head.

"Oh, come on!" said Abigail. "We're not going to let you go on your own. Foggy is our friend, too."

Finn smiled.

"Vale, you stay here with Elias and protect him if any of these guards wake up and give him trouble," said Finn. "Luxor, you come with Abigail and me."

"Me?!" shouted the robot. "Why?!"

"Because," said Finn. "You're our ticket inside."

Chapter Ten
Fireworks

"Oh, this is so exciting!" exclaimed Luxor as they left his house.

"Why are you so excited?" asked Abigail.

"Because!" Luxor answered. "In every great story about a knight or a warrior, they are sent on an impossible mission by a king or queen. And the hero must prove his or her worth by completing several trials. Luckily, in this story, there are three warriors. You two and me."

"We're not warriors," said Finn.

"You are now," said Luxor.

"And we weren't sent on a mission by the queen," said Abigail. "We're working against the queen."

Luxor lowered his voice to reflect the drama of the situation and said: "These are your trials."

Abigail rolled her eyes at Finn and laughed. If they were going to go on this impossible mission, they might as well have a robot narrator with them. They walked out into the alleys of the village, Luxor hovering just above their heads.

They tried to keep their eyes down and be as unnoticeable as possible.

"Okay, Luxor," said Finn. "Now, if we run into anyone who recognizes us, you need to tell them you've caught us. That way you get to be the hero for the queen, and we get into her castle without any trouble."

Luxor smiled and nodded. He seemed pleased with the plan.

"Walk a little stiffer, Finn," whispered Abigail. "Like your arms are made of metal."

Finn did his best to walk robotically. They'd already made it halfway through the village, and no one had raised a metallic eyebrow at them.

"It's working," he whispered. "No one suspects a thing."

"CLEAR THE WAY! CLEAR THE

WAY!" shouted Luxor above their heads. "VILLAINS COMING THROUGH. THAT'S RIGHT—I, LUXOR, HAVE CAP-TURED THE VILLAINS WHO ELUDED THE QUEEN'S GUARDS NOT SO LONG AGO! PLEASE MAKE WAY SO THAT I, LUXOR, MAY RETURN THEM TO THE QUEEN'S CUSTODY!"

Finn gasped. Abigail poked Luxor in the belly.

"Luxor! That's not helping!" she shouted.

"TELL YOUR FRIENDS, TELL YOUR ENEMIES THAT IT WAS I, LUXOR!" The robot was shouting to everyone in the village. "THE QUEEN HAS NO BETTER FRIEND THAN LUXOR. THAT'S L-U-X-O—"

"We better run now," Abigail told Finn.

But just then, a robot shaped like an upside-down pear floated in front of them, blocking their path.

Luxor stopped talking and he stopped flying. If a robot could go pale, Luxor would have been white as a sheet.

Finn recognized the strange-looking bot immediately. It had been at their dinner with Queen SuperAwesome when they'd landed. "I know them!" shouted the robot. "You're right, Luxor, you fool! You have captured the scallywags."

"Scallywags?" asked Abigail. "What are you, a pirate?"

"How dare you!" shouted the pearbot. "I am 212222122221111, chief chef of our world. I made you the little stone bricks you so rudely declined to eat!"

"I love a tasty stone brick!" said Luxor.

"Oh, be quiet, Luxor," said the chef. "I can take them in from here, cough cough."

"Hey, these are my prisoners," said Luxor. "And besides, this has to be our first trial."

"These fleshy creatures cannot go to the queen," said 212222122221111. "They must be brought to the dungeons!"

"Dungeons!" shouted Finn. "Why do robots have dungeons?"

"Yeah," said Luxor. "Why do we have dungeons?"

"Enough!" shouted the chief chef. "The

dungeons are the caves and tunnels that run below this village. They have always been there. We have been slowly filling them with black tar to reinforce our streets and buildings. But now we can fill them with you!"

212222122221111 reached down and grabbed Finn by the shoulder.

"Let's go!" the robot shouted. "I will *CUF-FAWFOFAFFFAFOFF.*"

"You'll what now?" asked Luxor.

But the chief chef couldn't answer. He took a step back and opened his mouth. Out poured a waterfall of sparks.

"Oh, he's got a bad case," said A

The chef coughed again, and a small, w

tling tube, almost like a tiny firework, shot out

of his ear.

"Uh," said Finn.

"Puke puke *pukity* puke," said the chef, and

a long, thin rocket shot out of his nose, up

into the sky, and exploded in a spray of sparkly

golden lights.

"The virus makes fireworks?" asked Luxor.

"It must do different things to different

robots," said Finn.

"*BLURPY!*" shouted the chef, and four

streaking fireworks flew out of his ears, up

above the village, and sent blue and green spar-

kles raining down on the rooftops.

"Oooohhh," said the robot villagers.

"They like it," said Luxor.

"No, this is bad," said Finn. "We need to

e else is going to come

and. He spotted another vat

d used on the guards. He ran

de of a building and grabbed a

hose, ng it off its faucet.

"Hey, that's vandalism!" shouted Luxor. "You heard the chief chef! They need that to fill the dungeons!"

"No, *that's* vandalism," said Finn. The chef was now hiccupping like mad and the fireworks were growing increasingly larger. If one rocket shot off in the wrong direction, someone could get hurt.

Finn put one end of the hose in the bucket and pointed the nozzle at the chef. There was a small lever on the side and he cranked it as hard as he could.

"Here we go!" shouted Finn.

Ploop.

A tiny squirt of goop came out the end of the hose, doing nothing more than dirtying the chef's toes.

The chef hiccupped and shot a rocket straight at Luxor. It bounced off the flying bot's round belly and crashed onto the ground nearby.

"I'm okay!" shouted Luxor. "But hurry up already! Really crank it!"

Finn pumped the lever on the hose as fast as he could. He then flipped it one last time, and a rush of goop flew out of the nozzle. It was like a firehose of disgusting black glue. But it did the trick. The goop put out the fireworks in the chef's belly, and the robot collapsed onto the ground.

"Our first trial is complete!" shouted Luxor. "The chef is defeated, and we may now proceed to the queen."

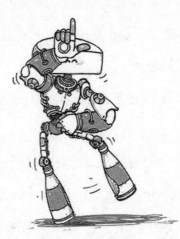

Chapter Eleven
Swarm and Cozy

Finn, Abigail, and Luxor raced out of the village. It's hard to stay hidden once you trigger a fireworks show in the middle of a town.

The two explorers ran as fast as they possibly could, until they were in the clearing separating the village from the queen's palace. The only thing between them and Queen SuperAwesome now was their explorer pod, which looked positively peaceful parked on the smooth stone.

"I really don't like battling these robots," said Finn.

"Why?" asked Abigail. "They don't seem to feel too bad about battling you."

"Yeah, but Foggy," said Finn. "I love Foggy. And he's a robot. And for some reason, all these robots have this idea that they're better than we are."

"Can you shoot fireworks out of your nose?" said Abigail.

"Ha-ha," laughed Finn. "Maybe if I drink enough soda. Anyway, Foggy just seems like such a different robot down here. We have to get to him so Elias can make him better, and then we'll take him home and figure it all out."

"But Finn, what if Foggy doesn't want to figure it out?" asked Abigail. "What if he wants to stay with his robot friends?"

"Then I will be really sad, and I'll eat like eight ice creams when we get home," said Finn as they passed the explorer pod. "But it doesn't matter. Because Foggy will want to come with us. I just know it, and— Oh, hey, that looks bad."

Finn's feelings had to wait. The robots were coming! How many of them were there? Thousands? Millions? Teeny-tiny

robots, the kind that bounced back when Finn stepped on them. They were swarming out of the palace and coming straight for Finn and Abigail.

"Oh, ew," said Luxor. "These little disgusting things."

Luxor flew up about ten feet above their heads.

"Good luck!" he said. "I'll just be up here."

"I thought you were a warrior!" shouted Finn.

"This is just the second trial," said Luxor. He flew farther away from the tiny robots. "I'll take care of number three. Promise."

Finn and Abigail had nowhere to go. They ran back to the explorer pod and climbed up on top of it. They needed to get up high.

The tiny robots were like a swarm of insects. The shiny stone ground turned black with them as they rushed toward the explorers.

"I don't see any weird goop around," said Abigail.

"Yeah, what are we going to do?" said Finn.

"Wait, shhh, listen," said Abigail.

The microbots were so small, their voices were barely louder than a whisper. But together, they grew louder. Tiny *blurb*s and coughs that added up to one big virus.

"They're sick, too," said Abigail.

"Ugh," said Finn. "What do we do now? We know stepping on them won't help. They'll just bounce right back."

"I have an idea," said Abigail. "It's weird, though. So you stay here, and if it doesn't work, make sure you still get to Foggy."

"What?" asked Finn. But Abigail was already gone.

She jumped down onto the ground just as the microbots reached the pod. The tiny robots paused for a moment, like a tidal wave right before it crashes. Abigail lay down on the ground and the swarm surged over her.

"Abigail!" shouted Finn. "No!"

Abigail was covered with so many little

robots, Finn couldn't even see her anymore.

"Abigail, can you hear me?!"

There was no answer. The microbots started to make their way up the pod's walls, too. They were going to overtake Finn at any moment. There wasn't much he could do. He could try to get into the pod and away from the swarm. Or he could do something crazy.

He knew if it were him down there, Abigail would do something crazy. So would Foggy.

He jumped down to where he thought Abigail was, and he could hear their little voices. They were spreading all over him. In between coughs, they were saying things like, "Ha-ha! Take that! And that! Who's stomping who now?"

But Finn also heard something else.

"Hahahaha."

It was Abigail's unmistakable laugh.

"That tickles."

Finn reached down and began sweeping microbots away, trying to find Abigail. He didn't want to hurt the bots, but he also needed to save his friend.

Finally, his fingers struck the glass of her space helmet. He cleared the robots away so he could see her face.

"It's okay, Finn," said Abigail. "I'm fine."

"But what are you doing?"

"I'm getting tickled," she said. "If I were a tiny robot, I think I'd get tired of being stepped on all the time. So what's the one thing that would make me feel better?"

Finn heard another tiny, whispered chorus of microbots. "Stomp stomp. Take that!"

"You'd want to stomp back," said Finn.

"Exactly," said Abigail. "They just want their tiny revenge."

Finn laughed. He lay down next to her.

"Have at it, tiny robots!" shouted Abigail. "You have defeated us!"

Finn couldn't stop laughing.

"You're a genius!" he shouted between chuckles. And the two of them lay side by side

as the microbot swarm passed over them, stomping away, tickling them the whole time.

"Okay, they're gone now!" said Luxor.
"You can get up. Weirdos."

Chapter Twelve
Trash Day

As Finn, Abigail, and Luxor made their way toward Queen SuperAwesome's palace, Finn heard a piercing scream. It came from the village behind them.

"AaaaaAAAAAAAAAHHHHHHHHH!"

"Up there!" shouted Luxor.

Some sort of hovering disc was flying

toward them. It had to be a robot. Finn and Abigail knew what real spaceships looked like. They lived on one, for crying out loud. And this disc did not look like a real space-ship. It was more like a cartoon flying saucer—round like a plate, with a small bub-ble in the middle.

As the disc got closer, the screaming grew louder. The robot wasn't screaming, of course. It was Vale. He was hanging from it upside down. And dangling from Vale's arms, also screaming mightily, was Elias.

"HELP MEEEEE!" shouted Vale as the flying robot neared Finn and Abigail. Elias was still going with the classic "AAAAAHHHH-HHHH!"

"What happened?!" shouted Finn as Vale and Elias came within a few feet of their friends. But they were much too high for Finn to grab.

The flying saucer hovered nearby, spinning around and around.

Elias and Vale spun like they were inside a washing machine.

"We were just coming to get you," said Vale.

"We fixed the guards," said Elias. "AAAH-HHHH."

"AAHHHH," agreed Vale. "And then we stopped to clean up that robot you covered in goop."

"YEEEAAaaaAHHHHH!" shouted Elias. "And then this thing came along and sort of vacuumed up Vale. Got him by the feet."

"But I don't fit!" shouted Vale. "So I'm *whoa*, stuck, *whoa*, halfway out."

"And I grabbed him!" said Elias. "But I can't pull him out."

"Okay," said Finn. "Luxor, is this the third trial?"

"Oh, sorry," said Luxor. He turned toward the explorers.

"Combatants!" he shouted. "Welcome to your third trial!"

"Cool," said Finn. "But we need to get Vale out of there before he's swallowed. Like, now. What do we do?!"

Luxor zoomed over to the flying saucer. He

reached up and pressed a button on the top of the bubble.

"*Boop*. Powered down," said the flying saucer.

It lowered down toward the ground, paused about ten feet in the air, and released Vale. Luckily, Elias was there to break Vale's fall.

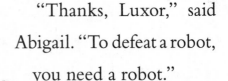

"Thanks, Luxor," said Abigail. "To defeat a robot, you need a robot."

"That wasn't even a robot, you chuckleheads," said Luxor. "That was a trash automaton. Basically, a flying vacuum. I'm insulted you thought that brainless appliance was a robot."

"Great," said Finn.

"The gang's all here. To the queen!"

"Wait a second," said Abigail. "We need a plan."

"The plan is to get Foggy out of there and get home," said Finn.

Elias put his hand on Finn's shoulder.

"But what if Foggy—"

"I know, Abigail already asked me that," said Finn. "If Foggy would rather be friends with these robots . . . then I have to let him stay. I'd have to be the kind of friend who cared more about his friend's happiness than his own."

"No," said Elias. "I was going to say, what if we can't fix Foggy? What if the virus is too strong?"

"Not an option," said Finn. "I have the best scientist in five galaxies here to fix Foggy."

"Oh, awesome!" said Elias. "Who?"

"You, buddy," said Finn. Elias was shocked.

"Finn, I'm seven," said Elias.

"That's a lucky number!" shouted Vale. "And this is boring. To Queen SuperStinky's palace!"

Vale and Finn dashed toward the palace in the distance.

"Come on, Elias," said Abigail. "No pressure."

She ran after Finn and Vale. Elias shook his head and sprinted to catch up.

"That trial was no fun," said Luxor. "What a rip-off!"

Chapter Thirteen
Long Live the Queen?

The explorers all rushed through the door to the dining hall where they'd left Foggy. There, Queen SuperAwesome sat at the head of the table. Her eyes were still closed. Her chin rested on her chest.

She was clearly still sick and unable to function.

A few of the other robots who had been at

the dinner were also still sitting at the table. If robots could look worried, these seemed desperate. One was nervously pressing three buttons on the side of its head. Another twiddled its antennae.

Finn rushed to the queen's side but tripped on something. Foggy was still beside her. He was just lying on the floor.

"No one even picked Foggy up?!" shouted Finn. "Come here, buddy."

Finn and Abigail picked up Foggy and laid him on the table.

"Elias, how did you make the robot guards feel better back at the village?"

"It was easy," said Elias. "I just had to do a simple reboot. Their numbers, the 1s and 2s, were printed on the inside of their panels. I just typed those in and the guards reset. They're good as new. I'm sure they'll be here any minute."

"Great," said Abigail. "Try that with Super-Awesome."

Elias bent the robot queen forward so her head was on the table. He peeled off her back panel to reveal the same type of keypad that was in the guards.

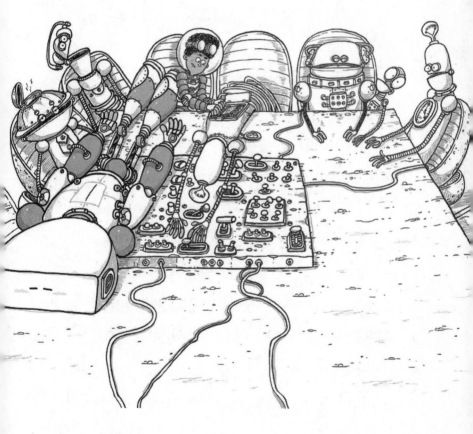

"There's no number here!" said Elias.

"Just try any combination," said Vale.

"There are probably billions of those," said Elias.

"Then try the one that's most superawesome," said Vale.

"Try 2111222111122121222," said Finn.

"Really?" asked Elias.

"Yeah," said Finn, and he blushed. "That's her name. I wanted to remember it. If she was going to be Foggy's new best friend, I wanted to be her friend, too."

"That is so sweet you would do that for the robot queen," said Elias. "Not a sentence I ever thought I'd say, but . . . here goes."

The queen beeped and booped, lights flickered behind her metal eyelids, and, after a few seconds, her head lifted.

"Get out!" she shouted. "Get out! All of you! Now!"

"Hold on," said Finn. "We just saved you."

"Yes," said Queen SuperAwesome. "After you brought that sick robot to our home. The second he plugged into the table I knew something was wrong. He gave me a virus so strong it shut down my entire system."

"Fair," said Vale.

"Just let me help my friend Foggy," said Finn. "And then we'll go."

"You are no friend of robots!" shouted the queen. "You probably gave him that virus!"

Finn's shoulders sunk.

"You're right, I did," he said. "But I didn't mean to. He got sick because he was trying to be a good friend to me. He was keeping me company when I was sick. And now I just want to make him better."

The queen seemed unconvinced.

"Hey, this may be a bad time," said Luxor. "But I just wanted to say hello, Your Majesty!

I'm the one who captured the flesh creatures and brought them back to you. You know, in case you were wanting to reinstate me as a friend of the Queen's Court."

"Oh, please," said Abigail. "We're the ones who brought you here. You wouldn't have lasted through one trial."

"Everybody out!" screamed SuperAwesome. "Guards! Take them to their ship! I don't want to see these humans ever again!"

Three new guards ran into the room and grabbed Elias, Vale, and Abigail. But Finn was down on his knees, trying to help Foggy.

"Let us go!" shouted Vale. "We're not leaving without all of us, including Finn and Foggy."

"No," said Finn. He'd taken off Foggy's back panel. "You should go."

A faint humming sound came from Foggy's back.

"You're kinda stealing my thunder here," said Vale.

The noise from Foggy grew louder.

"Finn," said Abigail. "What's wrong?"

"It's Foggy," said Finn. "I think he might explode."

Chapter Fourteen
Friends Don't Let Friends Blow Up

"Nonsense," said Queen SuperAwesome. "You don't know anything about robots!"

"Actually, Your Majesty, he does," said the chief chef, walking through the door. "He stopped me from exploding earlier. And his friend, the quiet one, saved the guards outside."

"Yeah," said Vale. "And I nearly got swallowed by one. So, you know, I learned a lot."

"Everyone be quiet!" yelled Finn. His face was red. Sweat pooled inside his helmet. "Foggy's in trouble. Elias, come here."

Elias peered over Finn's shoulder at Foggy's control panel. There, beneath a small keypad and a screen, was a glowing green light. Finn pushed back a few wires. The green light grew brighter. Some of the wires around it had melted.

"It's the battery, right?" said Finn. "It's overheating?"

"Yeah," said Elias. "He must have been really sick. Or sick for longer than any of us realized."

"But how could this happen?" said Finn. "Robots aren't affected by germs. They can't run fevers."

"Must be his processor," said Elias. "It's working overtime to try to clear out the virus."

"Because Foggy was working overtime to

help us when we were sick," said Finn. "If he hadn't cared so much, he never would have spent so much time with us. And I never would have gotten him sick."

Elias peered at the battery.

"Finn, if that battery overheats and cracks . . ."

The humming grew louder. The battery started to shake.

"Then Foggy could explode," said Finn.

The weight of it hit him like a tray full of smooth stone bricks. He couldn't let this happen to his best friend, but how was he going to stop it?

The battery vibrated. It looked like it was going to jump out of Foggy.

"Okay," said Finn. "So how did you cure the others? You typed their names into their keypads and reset them, right?"

"Yeah," said Elias. "But Foggy doesn't have a coded name like that. He's not 111212212122 or anything."

"He's just Foggy," said Abigail. "Our friend."

"Okay, so let's think of what it could be," said Finn. "What's the code to reset him?"

Finn felt like a surgeon. There was his friend, laid out on a table in front of him. The pressure from everyone hovering over him, watching and waiting, was impossible.

"You could try 36449," said Elias. "On a keypad with letters, that spells Foggy."

Finn typed it into the small keypad. Nothing.

A wisp of smoke curled up from the battery.

"You guys need to get out of here," said

Finn. "He could blow at any second."

"Never," said Abigail. She put her hand on Finn's shoulder.

"I am leaving, and I suggest all the other robots leave, as well," said the queen. "These flesh creatures don't know what they are doing. They know nothing about our kind."

SuperAwesome stood and ran out the door. The chef stayed. So did Luxor.

"Hey, I had an idea," said Luxor. "The last trial was kind of a dud. Maybe this is the final trial."

"Who cares about your trials right now?" said Vale.

"You could try 6275693," said Abigail. "That would spell *Marlowe*."

"Worth a shot," said Finn. He typed it in, but it didn't work. The battery darkened and turned a bright red. Now smoke was coming from the metal bracket holding the battery.

Finn grabbed it to try to hold it steady.

"Ow!" said Finn. The heat had burned his fingers through his spacesuit.

"I'm sorry, Finn, but we have to go," said Elias. "Now! The fluid inside that battery is combustible. It can burst into flames. If the battery cracks and the fluid leaks out and touches that metal, it'll explode. And this whole building will blow."

"I feel like I should be able to figure out this code," said Finn.

"It could be anything," said Elias. "It could be whatever the engineers on the *Marlowe* put in when Foggy was made."

"How am I supposed to guess that?!" said Finn.

"You can't!" said Abigail. "That's why we have to go."

"We have thirty seconds, max, before he

explodes!" shouted Elias. He stood up. "Guys, we have to leave."

His friends pulled on Finn's shoulders. They dragged him out the door and into the pink sunshine of the robot planet.

Behind them, the entire room glowed a bright red.

"I'm sorry, Finn," said Abigail. "I know he loved you."

"I love you guys, too," said Finn. "Remember that, you know, just in case."

"Oh no," said Vale. "He's about to do something stupid, isn't he?"

"You would know!" yelled Finn. He dove back into the palace.

Chapter Fifteen
Aftershocks

Elias, Vale, and Abigail ran for the explorer pod. The building was going to blow any second, and they had to get behind the pod before it did.

They dove behind their ship. But nothing happened. Just silence.

"Guys!" shouted Vale. "I think the explosion hurt my ears. I can't hear anything!"

Abigail shook her head.

"That's because there's nothing to hear," she said. She stood up and peered around the pod. There was Finn, dragging a very heavy Foggy out of the queen's palace.

"They're okay!" she shouted, and ran toward Finn.

Foggy woke up just as Abigail reached them.

"What are we doing outside?" said Foggy. "And why do I feel a breeze inside me?"

"Oh, sorry," said Finn. He reached back and shut Foggy's panel.

"Finnegan Emerson Caspian, I am very glad you're alive but now I have to kill you," said Abigail. "That was the dumbest, bravest, but mostly dumbest thing I've ever seen some-one do."

"Can you take his legs?" said Finn. "I think we're going to have to carry him to the explorer pod. He's a little weak."

As the troop made their way back to the ship, Abigail berated Foggy for being a bad friend to Finn.

"And we found you just lying on the floor!"

said Abigail. "Could any of your new robot friends be bothered to help you up? Nope! They just left you there like trash."

"Hey," said Vale. "Lay off of trash. I have a newfound respect for it."

"I know," said Foggy. "I know. It was ridiculous of me. I was so excited about these new friends, I stopped paying attention to my good friends, and then I almost met my end. Is that a poem I just wrote? My head hurts."

Abigail buckled Foggy into his seat and took the pilot's seat. She pressed the throttle and launched the pod up toward the *Marlowe*.

Finn sat next to Foggy.

"You must be very angry with me," said Foggy. "I don't blame you."

"Nah," said Finn. "I wasn't always great to you. My mom was right. I should have appreciated you more."

Foggy smiled at Finn.

"You know, we tried a couple different pass-codes to reset you," said Finn. "Your name and then your home."

All the explorers looked at Finn. They wanted to know how he'd saved Foggy.

"So I thought about how, if I were a robot and I had a reset code, I'd probably want to come up with it myself. And I'd make it something that I would never forget. Something that I really loved."

"3466," said Foggy.

"Yep," smiled Finn.

Vale looked down at the small communicator on his wrist.

"Let's see, 3-4-6-6," he said. "That spells 'dino.' That's weird. You love dinos?"

"Finn," said Elias. "It spells 'Finn.'"

Finn gave Foggy a hug.

"You know, Foggy," said Finn. "You're going to have to change your code now."

"Why?" asked Foggy.

"I think you should change your name," said Finn. "I'm thinking something like 12121222221112212211."

The pod zoomed toward the small purple light in the distance. The *Marlowe* was waiting for them, and Finn couldn't wait to get home and stay there for a while.

THE *FAMOUS MARLOWE 280* INTERPLANETARY EXPLORATORY SPACE STATION

HALL OF ALIENS

EXPLORERS TROOP 301 HAS VISITED MANY PLANETS ACROSS THE UNIVERSE. THEY HAVE MET, OUTWITTED, AND OUTRUN DOZENS OF ALIEN LIFE-FORMS. THESE ALIENS HAVE COME IN VARIOUS SHAPES, SIZES, AND BODY ODORS.

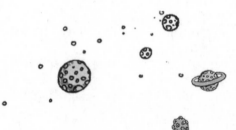

DOUG

Doug is a small alien with a big, glowing brain. He seems like he's your best friend at first, but that's just because of  the whole mind control thing. Doug is not to be toyed with. Doug is not to be trusted. Doug is, however, the Dougiest.

DEATH BUNNY

Sometimes a name just doesn't fit an alien. Sure, this alien looks like a bunny. And yes, he almost stole Troop 301's explorer  pod. And, of course, he did blow up an entire planet singlehandedly. But *death* bunny? That seems a little too extreme for a friendly and furry alien like this one!

ROCK GIANTS

They're big. They're dumb. They're crawling
out of the ground and they're coming for you.

SUPERAWESOME

Robots may not have
hearts. They may be just
a bunch of metal, wires,
and code. And they may
not be friendly if you
land on their planet.

But something Troop 301 has learned along the way: Give them a beat, and they'll dance to it. (Also, they will try to throw you and your friends in their weird robot dungeons.)

SAPHRITE

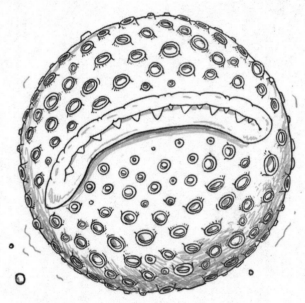

You know how your grandma is always telling you to eat more? And that a growing body needs a healthy appetite? And you practically have to dodge plates of food when you go to her house? That's what Saphrite's grandma was like. Except instead of food, Saphrite's grandma fed her planets. But, you know, same thing!

THE ALIEN ADVENTURES OF FINN CASPIAN

JOURNEY TO THE CENTER OF THAT THING

"Yeesh, I said *psssstt*," grimaced the beetle. "Don't you know what *psssstt* means?"

No one answered. They were too shocked by this enormous, talking beetle.

"It means keep things quiet, ya know?" said the beetle. "On the qt. The down low. Small ball. Mini talkie."

No one said anything, but Foggy and Vale flew down to the ground to investigate.

"See?" said the bug. "Even that. Too loud. You need to take it down a notch. Inside voices. Whisper misters. Soft vocals. The down low."

"You said that one already," whispered Abigail. "But why do we have to stay so quiet?"

The beetle seemed to laugh at this.

"Duh," it whispered. "So you don't wake up the boss. The big cheese. The head honcho. The top dog."

"And who is that?" whispered Finn.

"Who is the big kahuna?" asked the beetle. "The heavyweight? The muckety-muck and the luckety-luck?"

"Yes," sighed Finn. "Who is that?"

The beetle took another step out of the grass. Its body was even bigger than they expected. On another day, on another planet, Finn could probably ride it like a pony.

"You're telling me you don't know where you are?" asked the beetle. Everyone shook their heads. "You wanna know who the top banana is? You're standing on her."

The explorers all looked at each other, then down at the ground. The turf was rough and brown, but it wasn't that strange. They'd been on much weirder planets.

Vale picked up his foot and looked at the bottom of his shoe as if he were checking for dog poop.

"Is she like you?" asked Elias. "Is she a . . . um."

Elias caught himself. The beetle probably didn't think of itself as a bug.

"A bug?" asked the beetle. "No. Saphrite is not a bug. Saphrite is the planet eater, the colossus, the giant that all giants fear."

"I'm sorry," said Foggy. "Who is this Saphrite?"

"Yeah," said Finn. "And where is she, exactly?"

"Oh, I see," said the beetle. "You really don't know. Bubs, you're not standing on a planet. You're standing on Saphrite. She *is* this planet."

Blast off into more adventures inspired by the award-winning kids' podcast!